HELL

AND

DAMNATION

BY
CAROLYN GREGG

HELL AND DAMNATION
Copyright © 2012 by *Linda Mooney*
Print ISBN 978-1517016302

Cover Art: Ash Arceneaux

CHAPTER ONE

"Oh, *Barney!*"

The woman's scream of ecstasy couldn't have come at a better time. Danelius continued to ram his concrete-hard cock into her as Ingrid Dardin flailed on the bed. He could tell she was already reaching her peak. Her pussy was convulsing, trying to hold him inside her wonderfully warm and wet cunt, but Danelius had no trouble pumping her with jackhammer precision.

"Barney? Who the fuck is Barney!"

Well, it was about damn time! Mr. Dardin slept like the dead, and it had taken all this time for the man to finally wake up and realize his wife was in the throes of a major orgasm while dreaming she was with her lover.

Quickly, Danelius withdrew from the woman but remained invisibly floating above the bed to watch the interplay. He grinned, knowing that the best part of the job was the revelation.

Ingrid blinked in surprise as her husband reared up in bed to confront her.

"Barney Baker *next door?*" he practically roared at her.

"Aww, honey—"

"Don't you fuckin' 'honey' *me*, Ingrid! Tell me the truth! Are you screwing our next door neighbor?" Caleb Dardin demanded.

The man was incensed, as well as he should be. Mrs. Dardin had been shagging the retired electrical engineer for close to two months now. It was about time the husband found out.

"Caleb, sweetie." Ingrid reached for her husband, hoping to soothe his temper, but Mr. Dardin would have none of it. Good for him.

Angrily batting away his wife's open arms, he rolled out of bed, then turned to face her. "Who else have you been screwing, Ingrid? Jesus H.! No wonder you don't answer the friggin' phone half the time I call you!"

"Calebie, it's not like that." She tried again to console him, to no avail. She knew she was busted, and she knew Mr. Dardin wasn't stupid enough to fall for her excuses.

Satisfied his work was done, Danelius mentally placed another mark in his *Accomplished* column and slowly descended back into Hell to give his report to the boss.

* * * *

"Well, fuck! "

Torreon sidled across the locker room and leaned over Danelius's shoulder to see what had set the man off. A quick jab in the ribs got his friend's attention.

"Join the club, buddy. I'll lay even odds that summons is bad news."

Danelius glared at him. "What makes you the expert? It's just a summons."

"Then why are you so upset?"

"Bad timing, man. I just finished nailing Mrs. Dardin ahead of schedule. I was hoping to snatch a little R and R on the Riviera before the next assignment." Danelius grinned broadly. "I got a good tip a really nasty-loving rock star was vacationing there, and I was hoping to find out just how nasty she could be." Backhanding the summons, he added, "I'd rather have another assignment than a summons."

"Congrats on the nailing," Torreon nodded, "but the rumor mill says the Old Man has been nursing a particularly foul mood for the past year or so. The count has been low. Way, way low. And he ain't happy about it." He gave a wave at the parchment in Danelius's hand. "Think back. Could you have done something to piss him off?"

Piss off the Old Man? Danelius snorted. It didn't take much to get on the Devil's bad side. For the life of him, he couldn't even begin to guess what the summons could be about. But Torreon was right. It could be good news or bad. When you worked in Hell, you had about a fifty-fifty chance.

"Who knows? What would it matter, anyway?" Danelius commented as he folded the summons and slipped it into his locker, then pulled out the oils.

"Well, that's one reason why I'm glad I'm jus old-fashioned demon, and not an incubus." Torreon

"Any idea who might be your next job?"

"I'm hoping it'll be Coretta Barnes of Cincinnati, Ohio."

The oils smelled faintly of jasmine. Danelius knew women loved the scent of jasmine. Glancing down at his pecker, he did a few calisthenics with it, watching it rise and elongate, then deflate and shrink at will. That was what he liked about being an incubus. He could control all of his bodily functions, what few he had. And by being a sex demon, he had honed his skills, especially the use of his cock, to the point where he felt he was probably one of the best seducers of the Underground.

Hey, if pride was a sin, he was going to do his best to oblige.

He began to slather on the oil when a second parchment suddenly appeared before him. It was just like the first one that had coalesced earlier before his eyes, except this memo was smoking around the edges. Not a good sign. Inside, a single word appeared on the summons.

Now.

"Well, shit. Okay," Danelius muttered. After parking the bottle of oil back in his locker, he disappeared, reappearing in the boss's favorite Hell Hole in time to see two under demons going up in flames.

Ooohh, crap! The Old Man wasn't in a foul mood. He was in a tear-you-a-new-asshole mood. Which could put anything he pronounced somewhere in the range of twelve point nine on the Richter scale.

"Danelius!"

"Present." He swallowed his rising gorge and tried to look confident. It wasn't easy.

Satan frowned, which made the earth tremble slightly. "The Dardin case. What happened?"

Danelius tried to flash the Old Man an easygoing smile. He failed. "Do you mean, what happened that shouldn't have? Nothing! I did the old woman. Her old man got wind she was cheating on him. Wham, bam, so long, ma'am. Quick in, quick out, just like always. Perfectly executed. Another tally on the wall. Why?"

Satan growled as his scowl got noticeably darker. "Quick in and out, eh? Well, that explains why you totally fucked up your last assignment. And I'm not talking about fucking in the fucking sense!"

Danelius took a step back in surprise. "Pardon? What do you mean?"

"I mean you left in too big a hurry, you incompetent peabrain!" the Old Man roared. Behind him, flames shot upward to where they almost scorched the cavern's ceiling. The room was quickly filling with the acrid scent of sulfur—again, not a good sign. "Apparently Mrs. Dardin was able to convince her husband she was dreaming about some movie star. The oaf believed her, and they've made up. Which means *you* screwed up, and I'm not talking screwed in the screwing sense again!"

Danelius stared open-mouthed at the news. He'd screwed up? He left too early, and they'd made up?

"Wait a minute! There's no movie star that I know of named Barney!" he started to protest.

"*Enough!*" the Devil barked. "I don't care whether there is or not. What I do care about is results. *Results,* you teensy little prick. I'm talking about results that you haven't been showing recently."

"Wait a minute! What do you mean? I've been doing my job!"

I don't care what you *think* you've been doing," Satan fumed. "What matters is that you've proven you're not quite suited for your job."

"Hey, wait a minute—"

"Which means you're either not capable, or you're not interested in doing your best. Either way, screw-up, you're dead meat."

The threat wasn't implied. It was promised.

"Wait! *Wait!* " Danelius shouted. Visions of himself being barbequed flashed before him. Yes, there were definitely worse things than living and working for the Devil.

—

"You can't accuse me like this and not allow me the chance to redeem myself!"

"Re*deem* yourself?" Satan smirked. "Who do you think I am? I can do any damn thing I please!"

"Hey, I've been a good incubus!" Danelius argued. As long as he remained standing there, the better his chances were that he would somehow manage to get out of this mess. He crossed his fingers, hoping he could convince Beelzebub to give him another chance. "Go check my reports! Go back and review my conquests! My percentage of souls is high! Maybe ninety-five percent or higher!"

"Proud of your quota, are you?" The Old Man glared.

"Damn right!"

"Think your percentage is more than adequate?"

"I would put my percentages up against any of the other incubi!"

The dark cloud of doom descended once more over Lucifer's face. His long, spiked tail whipped around his legs like an insane serpent. Even his horns quivered with suppressed rage. "Your percentages may be extraordinary, you pile of shit, but your numbers are *inexcusable!* "

"But..." He tried to think, tried to find some reason why the Prince of Darkness would say such a thing, but his mind had turned to dust.

"What do you have to say for yourself, you lump of useless clay?"

Danelius tried to swallow but failed. He was dry, worse than parched, but there was nothing to drink in Hell. Even if he managed to find a cup of water somewhere, what *could* he say? Obviously the Old Man had made up his mind long before he'd summoned Danelius to his den. In fact, Danelius was beginning to think that it wouldn't matter if his numbers were at the top of the ranking. Satan had set his sights on him, and nothing on or under the earth would persuade the Father of Lies to think differently.

In fact, Danelius wouldn't put it past the Devil to have made up the whole thing in the first place, just so he could condemn his soul to the everlasting lowest pits of Hades. The Old Man was known for having done such a thing in the past, especially with people he'd previously had a run-in with. Or with people he didn't like for some reason or another. Or for no particular reason at all. It was not a nice thing to contemplate at seven o'clock in the morning.

Danelius knew he had few options left if he wanted to remain in one uncooked piece. He figured it was time to use one. Like groveling. Groveling was always a wise choice.

"Forgive me." It sounded lame, but it was a beginning. Sort of.

Satan raised one bushy black eyebrow in amusement. He was enjoying Danelius's torment, damn him. Too bad his mind was unreadable.

Danelius took a deep breath and plunged onward. "I do my job. I do it to the best of my ability. And I'm one of the best, if I do say so. Okay, so I lost a client. I'll go back and fix it."

"You're going to *fix* it?" The Old Man started to chuckle, but Danelius seriously doubted that the Devil truly thought he'd said something funny. "How do you plan to fix it? Go back and have her call out her lover's name again in the middle of another climax? Well, I hate to break it to you, dirt clod, but it won't happen. She's had a change of heart and already gone to her confessor. Your client has seen the error of her ways, meaning I've lost that soul. And there is nothing you can do now to remedy that. That means I'm now one soul short, condom boy! One. Soul. Short! And you know what *that* means, don't you?"

"No! No, not the Pits! I'm one of your best!" Danelius pleaded. Begged. To hell with groveling. It was time to get down and kiss the Old Man's taloned feet. "You don't want to condemn me to eternity in the Pits! You'll be making a huge mistake if you do!"

"Who are you to tell me I'd be making a mistake?" the Devil roared again. "I don't make mistakes!"

This was definitely not the time to remind Satan of his first and biggest mistake, which had condemned him to Hell in the first place. Nope, not the time nor the place. Danelius may be somewhat incompetent, but he wasn't stupid.

The best way to fight Lucifer's fire was with returning fire. After all, Danelius figured he had nothing left to lose.

"Give me an impossible mission," he challenged, straightening and facing the Old Man head-on.

The ruse appeared to work. Beelzebub actually appeared taken aback for a second. Danelius pressed on.

"Let me prove myself. Give me an assignment to make up for the soul I failed to deliver. Go on! I dare you!"

"*You dare me?*"

Ohhh, shit. Too late, Danelius realized he'd pushed too hard and too soon. Well, so much for pride.

Then, to his utter astonishment, Satan crossed his arms over his chest and began threading the fingers of one hand through his ebon beard. The air seemed to clear, and the smell of sulfur dissipated. If Danelius didn't know any better, he would swear his torment was amusing to the Old Man.

"Give you an assignment, eh?" the Devil repeated.

Anything he could grasp, any chance, Danelius was willing to take it. "Yes. Let me prove myself."

"Redeem yourself," Satan corrected. Danelius nodded, afraid of opening his mouth and saying anything else that would royally piss off the Old Man. Again.

"Very well. Here's your assignment. You're going to bring me a pure, innocent soul."

"I'm going to what?" Danelius thought he'd heard the Old Man wrong, but he didn't have the chance to ask any more questions. Before he'd taken another breath of rancid air, Danelius found himself standing smack dab in the middle of a road, on a freezing cold, rainy night.

And a pair of headlights were bearing straight at him, determined to run him down.

CHAPTER TWO

Danelius's first instinct was to vanish. The only problem was, he couldn't. Instead, a shiver ran through him, followed by a sudden rush of pure adrenaline. He leaped sideways, into the brush lining the side of the road, and painfully landed on his knees.

Behind him, a horn blared. There was a screech of tires as the car put on the brakes. Danelius ignored the vehicle and tried to fight the agony all around him. It was bad enough it was a wretchedly cold night, and rainy, to boot. But he was also buck naked, and landing in a thicket of thorns hadn't done him any favors.

To add insult to injury, he had fallen into something wet and slimy. For once, he was glad it was dark and he couldn't see what was oozing over his buttocks.

Dark, rainy, naked, and powerless. What else could go wrong?

"Hey, mister! Are you okay?"

Danelius vaguely recalled hearing the car door opening. What he didn't expect was for the driver to check up on him. A female driver.

"Hey!"

"I-I'm here! In the ditch!" he called back. He wondered if he should stand up or remain half-sitting, half-lying where he was. There was an unknown sludge making its way between his legs and slowly inching toward his balls.

"Are you okay?" the woman called out. Her voice was nearer, meaning she was searching for him. Danelius started to answer back when a beam of light suddenly caught him full in the face. He threw up his arms in defense. "Oh, geeze! Sorry!" The light dropped immediately. "I didn't hit you, did I?"

"N-No." He tried to shake his head, but the cold was permeating through his skin and beginning to freeze his blood. He opened his mouth to reassure her that she hadn't struck him, but speaking was no longer an option. His lips and tongue felt like they were frozen in place. He'd already lost all sense of feeling in his face and fingers, as well as in other areas of his body.

The flashlight roved over him. "Oh, good heavens! You're naked! What in the world are you doing out on a night like this without any clothes on?"

"I was dumped here," Danelius tried to explain, but the words came out sounding more like "I wa duh heah."

The woman climbed partway down the slope of the ditch and reached for him. "Come on. You gotta get someplace warm or else you're going to die of hypothermia."

Hypo-what?

The frigid temperatures were thickening the thought processes in his brain. Responding was impossible now. There was little Danelius could do or say as the woman tugged and pulled on him to get him into her car.

The interior of the vehicle was warm. As soon as she had him in the passenger seat, she shrugged out of her jacket and laid it cross his chest. Danelius gratefully clutched it while she slid under the steering wheel.

"I would take you to the nearest hospital, but the roads are too icy. Police are starting to shut them down," the woman told him. "You said you were dumped here? Were you kidnapped or something? Maybe you need to go to the police station."

"Wh-wh-whatever," he finally managed to say, leaning closer to the vents where heated air was gushing out. It didn't matter where she took him as long as it was some place where he could get warm again. He was aware of the woman staring at him, her eyes seesawing back and forth between him and the road.

"Aww, to hell with it," she mumbled, and turned the wheel.

They exited the main road onto a smaller one. Instead of big buildings sliding past the window, Danelius saw homes.

"Where're we going?"

"To my place. You need something warm inside you,

and I doubt you'll get any kind of help real soon at the police station. Besides..." She gave him another scrutinizing look. "If you were wanted by the police, you would have yelled bloody murder for me not to take you there. I'm pretty good at reading people, and something about you just punches my mothering button."

It was all he could do to nod. The heater in the car and the jacket were helping to thaw him out, but he was still in too much shock to notice.

He'd been thrown out of Hell. Wasn't that a trip? Booted by the big guy himself because Danelius had flubbed a mission. Hey! Wasn't Hell for sinners, anyway?

Either way, it didn't matter. Danelius knew Satan was notorious for going on tangents and pulling out some poor slob to rake over the coals. He'd just happened to be at the wrong place at the wrong time. Beelzebub had gotten the report about his screw-up, and it probably had been the capper on an already lousy morning. The proverbial last straw to set him off. As if the Devil needed an excuse to rip anyone a new asshole.

The woman pulled into a short driveway and parked underneath a carport. Hurrying around to the passenger side, she hustled him out of the car and into the small wood-frame house.

Once inside, she turned on the lights and disappeared down a hallway, reappearing a few moments later with a blanket, which she draped over his shoulders.

"Come sit down on the couch. I'll put a mug of water in the microwave to heat up. Would you like coffee or hot chocolate?"

She moved without any wasted movements, helping him into the next room and guiding him over to the sofa. A firm shove on his shoulders made him sit. She then tucked the ends of the blanket around him as she relieved him of the jacket. Next she clicked on a floor lamp as she passed it on her way into the kitchen.

Danelius stared at the room around him while his rescuer made them hot drinks. There was an overstuffed chair nearby. A basket of magazines and folded newspapers sat between. Everything looked innocuous. Simplistic. Comfortable.

"Did you say you wanted coffee or cocoa? I can also make some hot tea." The woman's voice drifted from the kitchen.

"Uhh, whatever's easiest," he managed to answer. Truth was, he'd never had either, so he was at a loss as to what he wanted.

Warmth was slowly spreading through his limbs. That, and weariness. The initial shock at being mortal was beginning to wear off. Danelius yawned, surprising himself.

The woman walked back into the living room. She carried two mugs of steam, one of which she handed to him. Danelius wrapped his hands around the ceramic cup and thanked her. The woman gave him a nod and a smile before taking a seat in the big chair.

After first sniffing the drink, he proceeded to take a swallow. Caustic acid scalded his lips and tongue. Danelius yelled. The hot liquid went flying, some of which landed on the blanket covering his thighs, and seeped through the material, where it burned his skin. Danelius jumped up as he yelled again, and the blanket slipped to the floor.

"Oh, my gosh! I'm sorry! I'm so sorry!" The woman was immediately on her feet, reaching for him. She managed to uncurl his hand from around the half-empty mug before taking it away.

Grabbing the blanket, she started to wipe away the steaming cocoa from his legs. "I should have told you it was hot. I'm sorry. Here. Let me go get some ice for that burn."

Standing in the middle of the living room, Danelius struggled to comprehend the sensations flowing over him. The pain was unlike anything he had ever experienced. Gingerly, he reached down to touch the red spots, when his eyes riveted instead on the empty space between his legs. His eyes widened in total fear, and he screamed. "Oh, shit! *Oh, shit!* My dick! Where's my dick?"

"What?" The woman came running back into the living room.

Danelius pointed to his groin. "My dick is gone! It

must have frozen and fallen off! We have to go back and get it!" He started for the kitchen door when he realized the woman wasn't moving to accompany him. Instead, he heard her giggling, which quickly turned to laughter.

Angrily, he took a step toward her. "Didn't you understand what I just said?" he almost growled at her.

She vainly tried to muffle her laughter, without success. But she did manage to catch her breath as she pointed to his package. "You-you're not... It's not gone," she finally was able to respond, although she continued to be plagued with another hearty set of giggles.

"What do you mean, it's not gone?" He glanced down at his crown jewels, minus. Instead of his penis predominately making itself known, there was a rather large dimple. "*Look* at me!" Danelius yelled. "I'm dickless!"

"No, no, you're not dickless," the woman continued to reassure him. "Come sit down."

"I have to go look for my dick!"

"No, you don't. Listen to me!" She gave him a little shake, forcing him to drag his eyes away from his crotch and up to her face. "Haven't you ever been cold before? Or gone swimming in very cold water?" she asked.

All he could manage was a shake of his head.

Smiling, the woman backed up. "What did you say your name was?"

"D-Dan-Danelius," he stuttered.

"Danelius. What an odd name. Well, hello. I'm Gemma MacKenzie. Good to meet you. Can I call you Dan?" She held out a hand, which he took, and they shook. "Okay, first things first. There's nothing wrong with you. It's a natural occurrence when a man comes in contact with sub-freezing temperatures. You still have your dick, Dan. It's just sort of tucked itself into your body to keep warm. Like a turtle going into its shell. Do you understand what I'm saying?" Gemma made a face. "Geeze, I can't believe I'm having to discuss male physiology to a grown man."

He looked back down at his new dimple. "It's still there? Then why won't it come out?" He gave his penis a firm order, but for the first time in his existence, his member refused to obey. "It won't mind!"

Gemma laughed again. "What do you mean, it won't mind? Oh, Dan, you're priceless. Here." She went back to retrieve the dishtowel she'd dropped, and gathered up the ice cubes she'd wrapped inside it. Bringing it back to the couch, she placed it on the burns on Danelius's leg. "There. How does that feel?"

"Better. Thank you."

"All right. Look, is there someone I can call to let them know where you are, and that you're safe?"

"Uhh, no."

Gemma gave him a wary look. "Where are you from?"

"Where am I from? I'm from Hell."

She blinked. "What?"

This time the cold felt good on his thigh where the hot liquid had burned him. Gingerly he readjusted the wrapped ice cubes over the redness.

"Dan?"

"Yeah?"

"Where did you say you're from?"

"I told you. I'm from Hell."

The look on her face went from amused to irritated. "Well, unless it's clearly marked on a map, I've never heard of the place," she commented sarcastically. "Here, I pick you up in the middle of the coldest night we've had so far this year, and you don't even have the decency to tell me where you live?"

He sighed. "I'm telling you the truth."

"That you came from Hell."

"To be precise, I got kicked out of Hell."

"Right," she nodded. However, her whole body language said just the opposite.

"I'm not lying to you, Gemma, even though lying in Hell is considered an attribute," he insisted, feeding off of her rising anger. "But this time I'm telling you the truth!"

She crossed her arms over her chest. "How does a person get kicked out of Hell? I thought people who did wrong *went* to Hell. Not got thrown out."

A shudder went through him. Immediately, Gemma

15

reached over to grab the blanket, lifting it back over his shoulders. The look of irritation turned back to one of concern. "I hope you're not coming down with anything."

None of it made sense to him. Not her comments. Not his being here. Not the fact that his body felt like it was no longer his to command. Not the fact that his dick had decided to play hide and seek without his permission. Nothing.

Suddenly, without warning, Danelius sneezed. He blinked in shock afterwards. "What was that?"

"What was what? You mean sneezing?" She reached over and placed a hand on his forehead. "You don't feel like you're coming down with a fever, but just in case I'll give you some acetaminophen. Look, Dan, all kidding aside, is there someone I can call to let them know you're here?"

He shook his head. "No. No one."

"Well, it's late, and the roads are getting worse by the minute. No telling what they'll be like in the morning." She gave him another cautious look. "If I let you sleep on the couch tonight, do you promise to be a good boy and not go wandering around the house? I have a can of mace and a baseball bat I plan to keep by my bed tonight, just to let you know."

Although he had no idea what a can of mace or a baseball bat was, they didn't sound like they would be pleasant to experience should he breach her confidence. "I won't go anywhere," he told her.

"You promise?" As soon as she'd said the words, Gemma rolled her eyes. "Listen to me. Asking someone who says he's been kicked out of Hell if he'll keep a promise. But...then again, maybe someone kicked out of Hell *would* keep a promise. Arrggh!" She shook herself. "Now you almost have me believing your malarkey! Hold on. Stay right there."

Danelius watched as she left the room, turning to go down the hall instead of heading back into the kitchen. A minute later, she reappeared with a few items.

"You can't keep running around in your birthday suit, I don't care who you are. Here." She handed him a baggy t-shirt and a pair of sweatpants. "They might be a bit small on you, but they're the best I can do in a pinch. At least they'll help keep you from further freezing your butt off. Hey, are you hungry? Would you like for me to fix you a sandwich or something?"

Danelius shrugged. "Am I hungry? I don't know. I don't know what hungry is." He frowned slightly at her. "This is strange to me, being mortal. It's confusing. And it hurts."

"Maybe what you need is just a good night's sleep. I'm bushed myself. Listen, the bathroom is down the hall, first door on the right. I'll go get you a pillow and another blanket while you get dressed."

She left, and Danelius took it as his cue to slip on the red sweats and white t-shirt while she was out of the room. When Gemma returned, she gave him an approving smile. "Nice. Not too snug, are they?"

"Snug?"

"The waistband." Lifting up the t-shirt, she slipped a finger inside his pants. The feel of her warm skin on his created an unexpected spark of desire that shot in two directions at the same time, tingling his toes and making his nipples perk up. His breath caught in his throat as he tried to grasp the sensation. Gemma didn't appear to notice.

"Mmm, the elastic has plenty of give. Good thing you have a flat stomach and slender hips, or else these pants wouldn't fit. Of course," she giggled, "you are a tad taller than me."

He glanced down to see what she was implying. The stretch cuffs circled his calves. He started to say something when she vanished down the hallway again, returning shortly with what looked like stockings.

"There's no way your feet can fit into a pair of my socks, but these leg warmers should work," she said as she tossed them at him. "Tomorrow I'll take you over to the police station, and we'll let them try and figure out who you are." She snorted, adding, "Kicked out of Hell. That's a good one. I have to admit, I haven't heard that one yet. Gotta hand it to you, Dan. You're original."

She left him once more, this time for a while longer.

When she finally returned to the living room, she was carrying a quilt and a pillow. After dumping the items on the couch, she held her hand out to him. "Here's the acetaminophen I promised. If you need water, help yourself to a glass in the kitchen. Are you sure you're going to be all right, Mr. Misfit?"

The jab managed to rouse him from his growing drowsiness. With the adrenalin fading, and the warm clothes snugly enveloping him, Danelius was finding it difficult to keep his eyes open. The fact that he was getting sleepy wasn't as surprising as the realization that he was actually going to go to sleep—something he had never done before in his entire existence.

Taking his silence as an affirmative, Gemma smiled once more. Good night, Dan. See you in the morning. Uhh, and don't forget what I said about the mace and baseball bat." Flashing him a final smile, she disappeared down the hallway, this time not to return.

Dully, Danelius stared at the two tablets lying in his palm. What was he supposed to do with them? What did water have to do with it? Furthermore, he was quickly getting to the point that he could barely stand up. Collapsing onto the couch, he reached for the quilt, wrapping himself in it. Lying down across the sofa, he turned his back to the light and closed his eyes.

He fell asleep almost instantly.

CHAPTER THREE

The moment she was out of range from the man, Gemma grabbed the telephone from the bedside table and tried to dial out. The sound of silence told her the lines were down. She had no luck with her cell phone, either.

"All available lines are in use. Please try your call again later."

She mentally screamed at the phone, including all the idiots who were trying to call whomever they believed were important enough to notify that they were stuck in traffic. Or stuck at work. Or, in her case, stuck with a guy who could be an escapee from the mental ward at some hospital. Of course, the simple realization that she was also one of those idiots clogging up the lines never occurred to her.

A dropout from Hell? Really?

She briefly wondered if either of the two hospitals in town had psycho wards. Surely, there had to be at least one or two nut cases who had to be kept strapped down in their beds. But would a guy who had lost all sense of reality actually walk around in his birthday suit on a night like this?

Maybe he had some clothes on, but somehow they got lost. Or misplaced. Or maybe he was mugged and had his clothes stolen. It would explain why he seems disoriented. Or maybe I'm just going way too far out on a limb for this guy.

She parked herself on the edge of the bed. Now what should she do? The guy seemed harmless enough, but she had seen too many horror movies to know he could be some crazed killer.

Gemma glanced over her shoulder, toward the bedroom door. But Dan didn't give off any vibes like that. In fact, she would swear he was exactly as he claimed—a guy who was lost and very uninformed about the real world. *Still, girl, it's better to be safe than sorry.*

Just her luck, he had to be cute. Maybe a tad scruffy,

but he was built. *Oh, my gawd, was he built. The abs, the arms, the pecs, the shoulders, the thighs.*

And the dick. She smiled. *Oh, yeah.*

She had a personal way of measuring a man's endowment, even if it was deflated and partially tucked away. She went by head size. If the crown was a decent size on the down side, she knew the whole would be more than adequate when it mattered. And Dan's little turtle had already gotten her silent check of approval.

"Just your luck, Gemma. You always did attract the oddballs."

She strained her ears and listened for any sounds coming from the living room. There was nothing, but that didn't mean the guy couldn't be tiptoeing right this moment down the hallway.

A little voice inside her head scolded her for not getting the lock on the bedroom door fixed when she'd bought the small house a few years ago. It was one of many little things on her To Do list she'd started when she'd moved in, and one of the many little things she had yet to get to. Damn her procrastination. But in all the time she'd lived here, how many times had she needed to lock her bedroom door?

After getting up, she went to her dresser and pulled out a necklace from the bottom of her jewelry box. It was a simple red satin rope with a huge jingle bell tied to the bottom. A holiday necklace she only wore around Christmas time. She draped it over the doorknob as a makeshift alarm. Hopefully, if he tried to get in, the thing would awaken her in time to grab the bat and mace.

Speaking of...

She pulled the bat from her closet and spray from her purse, setting the canister on the bedside table, and propping the bat between the table and the bed. Having them there gave her a greater sense of safety.

She glanced again at the door. Normally, she considered herself a good judge of character. Most of the time she could tell when someone was bullshitting her, and when they were trying to wheedle something out of her. For some reason, however, she was certain this guy was doing neither. He truly believed he was a minion from Hell, and that he'd been ejected for not doing his job. He'd never asked for her help, nor had he tried to come onto her. He was, for all intents and purposes, a poor slob who was wandering about in freezing weather with nowhere to go.

"Yep. Definitely a mental case."

But not all mental cases are dangerous...are they?

Fortunately, the lock on the bathroom door still worked. Grabbing her pajamas, Gemma first checked outside her door before slipping through the hallway and into the bathroom without hearing anything moving or rustling from the living room. Not even snoring.

Wonder if the poor guy sleeps like the dead?

She enjoyed the hot shower. She even washed her hair. If the phone lines were down, she knew it was only a matter of time before the electricity went out, too. Thank goodness the water heater, as well as the stove and clothes dryer, ran on gas. She'd once endured eighteen days one winter without electricity, and although she hadn't been too hard pressed, she nearly went out of her mind with boredom.

She sneaked back into her bedroom, but by now her curiosity was too much to bear. Was the guy still on the couch? Or was he up and prowling around?

After lighting a votive candle she kept on her dresser, Gemma softly padded barefoot into the living room. In the candle's dim glow, she could tell the man was still on the sofa where she'd left him. His back was to her, and his breathing sounded okay. She resisted the urge to place a hand on his forehead to check his temperature, afraid that it would awaken him. And the guy obviously needed the rest. As she'd suspected, he was sleeping like the dead.

Dead. From Hell.

This time she got the punch line and almost giggled. All right. Since he was out like a light, chances were he wasn't going to go snooping around the place after she turned in. Neither did she believe he was planning on coming after her to fulfill some sordid agenda. Maybe she'd get a decent night's sleep after all.

Crawling underneath the covers, already toasty, thanks to the electric blanket, Gemma smiled but made sure the bat was within easy reach.

Sordid agenda.

What about a mutually agreed upon sordid agenda?

Gemma, get your mind out of the gutter.

Unfortunately, her body was already humming to the possibility. Sex with a total stranger, and one as hunky as Dan? *Be still, my beating heart.*

In her mind's eye, she remembered the sight of his turtle's head snugly withdrawn inside his scrotum, and the thought of it triggered another realization.

The man had no body hair. Other than what was on top of his head, there was none on his chest or private area. And although she hadn't paid attention to them, she would bet there wasn't any in his arm pits, either. *What about his legs and arms? Would he have a shadow in the morning?*

He said he was mortal. Of course, he'll have a shadow in the morning.

Gemma, quit arguing with yourself and get some sleep. If the roads are closed tomorrow, it's going to be a long day with your new houseguest.

Pulling the bat into bed with her, she closed her eyes, feeling a lot more secure but just as confused about the man lying unconscious on the living room couch.

CHAPTER FOUR

Funny smells were coming from somewhere. It wasn't the odors that kept him awake once he drifted into consciousness, but the irritating gnawing sensation in his belly. And cramping. The pain hurt something fierce, and Danelius had no idea what could be wrong with him.

Then again, because he had never been mortal before, there could be any number of causes for his discomfort, he admitted to himself.

Sighing, he rolled over, and fell onto the floor. The quilt he was wrapped in managed to soften the short fall, but the unexpected landing was enough to wake him fully.

Gemma rushed into the living room to find out why he had yelled. Pausing in the entryway, she burst out laughing. Danelius managed to return the sentiment with a glare.

"You seem to get a lot of pleasure out of my discomfort and ignorance," he mumbled, getting to his feet.

"I'm sorry, but you looked so pathetic lying there, looking like a pig in a blanket." She muffled her giggles with one hand, but her eyes continued to sparkle with amusement. Danelius noticed they were blue eyes, and quite pretty. In fact, in the soft gray morning, he could better see all of Gemma MacKenzie. At least, the part that was visible above the red and white flannel pajamas.

She had short, reddish-brown hair and a smattering of freckles across her nose. And if she wasn't one of the most beautiful women he had ever seen in his eons of life, Danelius was hard pressed to think of anyone else whose looks came close. Even Helen of Troy had bad teeth. And Cleopatra...

He gave a little huff as he mentally wrote off the petite Egyptian.

"What?" Gemma asked. "Are you okay? I'm sorry I laughed."

"Nah. I'm fine," Danelius said. "I was just thinking of someone."

"Someone?" Her eyes widened. "Someone you know? Someone you can contact to come get you?"

He shook his head. "No. She died quite a while back."

"She?" This time a funny gleam passed behind those azure eyes. Danelius wondered if he'd imagined it. "You-your mother? Or, umm, girlfriend?"

This time it was he who laughed. "Girlfriend? Oh, goodness, no. But you reminded me of her."

"Oh?" The single word implied more, but Danelius was in the dark. Damn it, he wished he had his powers back. Then he could just look inside her soul and tell what she was thinking. What she was wishing. What she was hoping for.

Instead of pursuing the topic, Gemma turned around and went back into the kitchen. Throwing the quilt on the sofa, he followed her.

There was food cooking in the oven. He stood near the table and stared in amazement as she opened the oven door to extract a pan of items. The good smell was stronger now, and his stomach did some more of that agonizing clenching thing.

"It's not much," Gemma apologized. "Just some canned cinnamon rolls. I need to get to the store, but we had over five inches of snow fall last night. The roads are gonna be blocked at least until noon. How do you like your coffee?"

She had walked over to the counter to pour them two cups. The sight of her with the mugs reminded him of his scalding the night before. Danelius backed up out of reach while keeping a wary eye on her. Gemma appeared not to notice his reluctance to come to the table.

"You know, I was thinking about last night. You were damn lucky I came by when I did. I mean, I normally don't stay late at work. But since it was Friday, I didn't want to have that report waiting for me to finish first thing Monday morning. No, I told myself to go ahead and get it done and over with. That way I could relax and enjoy my weekend, without that worry hanging over my head like a dark cloud."

As she rattled on, Gemma iced the hot cinnamon

rolls, then placed the pan on the table. She pulled back her chair and started to take her seat when she finally noticed him standing near the back door.

"Oh, I'm sorry. I meant to ask you. Would you like some orange juice, too? It's pulpless."

He managed to shake his head, overwhelmed by all the things going on. Yes, he had been in kitchens before. In fact, he had a very nice memory of an encounter on a kitchen table much like this one. But in all of his existence, Danelius had been blind and numb to the sights, sounds, and especially the smells of humanity.

Suddenly, as a human mortal, he was vulnerable to every aspect of a life he had never known even existed before now. He could almost taste the sweet cinnamon. Or the hot aroma of the coffee. The sunlight shining in thin, weak shafts through the kitchen window over the sink still managed to light the room in a riot of colors. Reds, blues, brilliant whites—the hues almost screamed for his attention. The floor was bone-chilling cold. His stomach knotted in what he was beginning to understand were pangs of hunger.

To make things more complicated, now he felt an anxious need to...what?

Danelius unconsciously crossed his legs as he reached down to cup himself with one hand. Gemma frowned at him.

"What's wrong? Oh!" A pinkish sheen flared across her cheeks. "Go ahead and use the restroom. I'll wait for you."

"Restroom?" A room to rest in? Isn't that what he had done last night?

The need to do *something* continued to send signals to his brain. Confusing signals. Danelius winced. If Satan was going to make him mortal, the least he could do was to include a set of instructions to go with it.

"I...I..." As if being hungry and uncomfortable wasn't enough to contend with, now his body was sending him other messages he had no idea how to interpret.

"Dan, what's wrong? You're acting funny."

"I don't know what's wrong with me," he confessed in a tight voice.

Gemma got up from her chair and hurried over to where he was standing. "You're acting like you have to go to the bathroom." She blinked at him and took a step backwards. "Oh, come *on!*"

He managed to give a single shake of his head. "I've never been mortal before—"

She grabbed his arm by the elbow and led him down the narrow hallway to an open doorway. Stopping him in front of the toilet, she lifted the seat and pointed to the bowl. "I don't know what's going on inside that head of yours, Dan, but surely you know how to pee. Just don't expect me to hold you while you do."

She started to leave, but she paused when he asked, "How do I do it?"

The pinkish tinge on her cheeks now infused her entire face with a bright, almost ruby red color. Yet something in the tone of his voice must have touched a nerve. She gave him a look of astonishment.

"You're for real, aren't you? You *don't* know!"

"Please?" The pressure was building up to a point where he knew something was bound to happen. And it didn't promise to be pleasant.

"You, uhh..." She mimicked reaching inside her pajama bottoms and pulling out her hand, then pointing it downward. "Take it out and aim for the water in the bowl. When you're done, flush and wash your hands. Simple. Guys have it too easy."

She was out the door before he could reply. Quickly, Danelius reached inside to find his dick lying limp but present.

Well, hell, she was right! It didn't freeze and fall off!

He was surprised by the stream of water coming out of his member. But now was not the time to question this feat of mortal physiology. Nor the fact that the pressure in his abdomen was being relieved. After washing his hands as he had been ordered, Danelius returned to the kitchen.

"Feeling better now?"

"Yes. Thanks." He slid into the chair across from her. Mimicking her moves, he raised a glass to his lips. It had a tart but not unpleasant taste when he took a tentative swallow of the liquid.

The glass of orange juice was beaded on the outside with moisture. Danelius stared at his handprint outlined in the wetness with amazement.

"Okay, I think it's time you stopped this little act you've got going and come clean." Her voice was acidic, her tone harsh enough to strip paint.

Danelius glanced up to see his host glaring at him over the platter of cinnamon rolls. The defiant glitter in her eyes made her all the more appealing, making him hard-pressed to get angry with her in return.

"Little act?"

"I've heard of people losing their memories, but *no*body forgets how to pee!"

"I didn't forget," Danelius responded. "I never learned how."

"Never learned *how?*" Her shocked expression would have been funny to behold if she hadn't been so furious. "How in the world does a grown man not learn how to pee?"

The caustic question irked him. Frowning, Danelius replied. "Until last night, I've never been mortal. So when would I have needed to learn?"

"Oh, *bull*shit!" Gemma cried out, throwing a small towel at him. She missed, but not by much. "Couldn't you at least tell me the truth? After all I did to save your ass from freezing last night. I brought you here, and gave you a place to sleep. After all I've done, why are you still insisting on being such a jerk?"

"I've told you the truth, Gemma!"

"Oh, yeah, right. You were kicked out of Hell. *Ha!*" She got up from her chair so abruptly, it almost fell backwards. Regardless, Gemma ignored it as she hurried out of the kitchen.

Danelius stared at where she had disappeared. He was at a loss as to what he needed to do next. He had never been good at telling the truth, just as he had never been a very good liar, either. It was clear Gemma was peeved at him, but he was at a total loss at what he was supposed to do. If he still had his powers, it would have been simple to disappear for a length of time until she got over it. However, that was no longer an option.

What was he supposed to say? Where was he supposed to go?

He glanced down at his plate and the cinnamon roll sitting on it. It smelled good, if he was interpreting correctly what his senses were relaying to him. After poking at the roll, he pulled back a forefinger covered in icing. Curious, he licked the icing.

Umm. It was good.

He had no idea why it was good, or why he liked the taste, but that didn't matter. The rumbling in his mid-section increased with this new discovery, and so did the tightening in his belly.

Danelius began devouring the roll when Gemma stomped back into the kitchen. She appeared to be thoroughly disgusted. More so than when she'd left. Shaking the object she held in her hand, she muttered a couple of obscenities Danelius had used himself, except for different reasons.

"Fuck! Fuck! Damn it to hell! Wouldn't you know it?" She looked up at where he sat with his mouth half-stuffed with roll, and pointed the object at him. "You had something to do with this, didn't you?"

Unable to answer, Danelius pointed to himself and lifted his eyebrows in answer.

"Yeah, you! You made it snow so hard, they've closed the roads. There's no way anyone is getting anywhere until the plows come through. And there's no telling how long that might take."

By this time he had managed to swallow. "I'm sorry, but I'm not directly responsible for the weather. Especially not snow. My boss is more into heat."

Gemma remained standing near the doorway, staring at him with an indecipherable expression on her face. It was hard to return her stare, knowing she thought he was to blame for the weather conditions outside.

He glanced out the window over the kitchen sink.

Although it was daylight, the overcast sky made it appear gloomier. A thought struck him. How could he be so sure he wasn't responsible for the bad weather? At least in part, if not in whole? Who could tell what the Old Man could and would do if he got angry enough?

For that matter, how could Danelius be certain he was the only person cast out of Hades?

The unexpected thought surprised him. What if a lot more souls had been condemned to mortality? What if there were others out there like him?

Danelius rose from his chair and proceeded toward the living room. Gemma stepped aside to watch him pass. "What are you doing?" she asked.

"I don't know. I'm...I don't know who I am. I don't know what I'm supposed to be doing. This is all new to me. And, frankly, I'm scared out of my skin. But you're right. I can't stay here. I have to go find out if there are others who were kicked out like I was. I have to find out what I have to do with myself." He turned to face her. "How do people live? What makes them go on day after day?"

Gemma frowned in puzzlement. "What do you mean, how do people live? They just do. They get a job so they can get a place to live. So they can buy food and clothes." She slowly shook her head. "My God, you really *don't* know anything, do you?"

"I told you. I pissed off the Devil, and he condemned me to mortality. And until I fulfill his command, I'm forced to remain here." He stared down at her slight figure. Being a head taller than her, he could look down and see the soft swells of her breasts inside the neckline of her pajamas. Blue, fuzzy slippers barely poked out from below the hem of her pants. It wouldn't take much effort for him to lean over and gather her into his arms. If he did, he bet she would feel as soft and cuddly as she appeared.

Gritting his teeth, Danelius reached for the doorknob leading to the carport when Gemma stopped him.

"What do you think you're doing?"

"I cannot impose upon you any further. You don't want me here, so I have to go."

He brushed aside her hand and opened the door. A blast of frigid air struck him full-on, nearly driving him backwards.

Gemma took charge, pushing him aside to close the door. "If you think I'm letting you go out there in sub-zero weather without a coat or a pair of shoes on, you're crazier than I think you are. Go back to the kitchen."

"But—"

"Shut up and go back to the kitchen, damn it. Give me a chance to think this out." She made shooing motions at him, adding, "As if I didn't spend enough time last night trying to make sense of this shit."

She followed him back to the table where she waited for him to take his seat before sitting herself. For a long minute, they stared at each other across the short expanse. Slowly, resolutely, he watched her face soften until she gave a deep sigh and reached for her glass of juice.

"I give up."

"Why?" Danelius asked. He had no idea why she was giving up. Or what she was giving up. But it was clear she was no longer interested in staying mad at him, and at least that much was good.

"Because just when I think I've got your scam figured out, you go and pull something like that."

"Something like what?"

"Pretending to head off in the cold, dressed as you are."

He shook his head. "I wasn't pretending."

Gemma sighed again. "Yeah, I figured." She shot to her feet. "I need coffee. Would you like a cup? Do you drink coffee?"

"I've never had any," Danelius admitted.

"Never had any? First cocoa, then juice, and now coffee? What? They don't drink anything down where you came from?" Rolling her eyes, she slapped her forehead with the palm of her hand. "Sweet heavens, listen to me. I sound like a believer." She said no more as she poured two cups from the coffeemaker and brought them to the table. Handing Danelius his, she sat back in her chair across from him. "There's creamer and sweetener on the table. Go ahead and experiment. See what it takes to get it the way you like it."

Instead, he watched as she dropped the contents of some packets into her mug, then stirred the liquid until it was a pale brown color. He copied what she'd done. The results didn't taste too bad.

"All right. Since we're stuck here, want to give me the whole story?"

"What whole story?"

"Tell me about Hell," Gemma halfway ordered him. "Tell me what you did there, and why you got kicked out."

"Can I have another roll first?" he asked hopefully.

"Help yourself." She waved at the platter sitting between them.

He quickly stuffed part of a roll into his mouth before she changed her mind. "What do you want to know about Hell?"

"Well, is it hot?"

"Yeah. Damned hot."

She made a sound like she didn't believe him, but that was okay. Most people didn't whenever he had to tell them who he was.

"You said your name was Danelius? What's your last name?"

"Last name?"

"Yeah. It's usually your father's last name."

Danelius shook his head. "I don't have a father. I don't have a last name."

"What about your mother? You had to have a mother," she argued.

"Demons don't have mothers," he told her.

Her eyes widened. "Demons? What kind of demon?" Her gaze raked over him. He could see how she was thinking back to when she'd almost run him down with her car. He had been naked and vulnerable, and freezing his nuts off. Obviously appearing nothing like the kind of creature she believed demons should look like.

"I'm an incubus. Or I was," he quickly amended.

"An incubus?" She gave a bark of laughter. "A sex demon?"

"Yes."

His sincere tone of voice stopped her from laughing again. She took a sip of coffee. He did the same. The stuff tasted better as it cooled off.

"Go on. Keep talking."

"What else do you want to know?"

"Well, if you were already condemned to Hell, how did you get kicked out? I mean, I thought Hell was for those people who were bad. If you're bad, how do you get so bad, you get kicked out?" Gemma winced. "I mean, do you get thrown out if you're *good?*"

"I got kicked out for failing my last mission."

"Oh? You mean you had a job?"

"I told you," Danelius repeated. "I was an incubus. And I, uhh...I pissed off the Old Man."

"Old Man? You mean the Devil?"

"Yeah."

"You pissed him off because you failed your mission? Is that what you said?"

He gave her a small smile. "I also back-talked to him. Not a wise thing to do when he's already angry."

"Why was he already angry?" Gemma asked. She pulled her legs up into her chair, bringing her knees nearly up to her chin. For the first time Danelius realized he hadn't been thinking about bedding her. His body hadn't readied itself to screw her. In fact, he felt no need whatsoever to get between her legs.

What was wrong with him?

Swallowing hard, he tried not to think further about it. "Who knows? It doesn't take much to make Satan angry. You learn to stay out of his way when he is."

"Except you got caught."

Danelius scratched his chin. There were some spiky little hairs growing there, and they itched like crazy. "My job is to seduce women who are having affairs. I go in at night while they're asleep and screw them silly, and make them dream they're with their lover until they call out his name.

My job is accomplished when their husbands or current boyfriends wake up and realize the name she's calling out isn't theirs. And they end up having a huge fight and splitting up because of her infidelity."

Gemma lowered her legs, crossing one ankle over her knee instead. Danelius got a brief glimpse of skin between the buttons of her pajama top when she moved. For a moment, he wondered if her breasts were small or round. Or if their tips were dark colored or light. Something in his groin moved in response, surprising him.

"Are you telling me your job is to split up people by revealing the fact that a woman is having an affair?"

"When the woman sins, it's my job to bring her sin to light. I have to condemn her soul."

"What if it's the man who sins?"

"That's for a succubus to handle."

She took another sip of coffee while keeping an eye on him over the rim of her mug. "So you, uhh, your job is to screw these women who think you're their lover? And when their husbands find out they've been hoodwinked, you collect their souls for your boss?"

"That's pretty much it."

"Um-hmm. And what do you get out of it?"

He looked up from where he had been staring at the last cinnamon roll. "What? Get out of it?"

"Yeah. How do you get paid? You do get paid, don't you?"

"What would I be paid with? What would I buy?"

"Hell, I don't know!" Gemma exclaimed. "A pack of gum? A packet of briefs?"

"Briefs?"

"You know. Underwear. Clothes."

"We don't need clothes in Hell, Gemma," Danelius told her matter-of-factly.

She gave another snort of disbelief. He continued to eye the cinnamon roll until she told him he could have it if he wanted it. Happily, he snatched it up.

"You said you had another mission," she reminded him.

"Umm?"

"You said something about having to fulfill a contract or something, and then you could go back to Hell. Did I understand you correctly?"

He licked his fingers. "I have to make up for the soul I failed to get on my last job."

"How are you going to do that?" Gemma asked.

"I haven't figured that out."

"Where are you going to stay? How will you eat?"

"I haven't figured that out, either."

"Well, what *do* you know?"

He sighed loudly. An unexpected bubble of air rose from the center of his body, and made a rather loud sound when it exited his mouth.

"Excuse you," Gemma said.

"What?"

"You burped. Or rather, you belched. In polite society, you cover your mouth and say, 'Excuse me'."

"Excuse me."

"Now, you were saying?"

"That's pretty much everything. I'm an incubus. I fucked up my last assignment, and Beelzebub was already in a foul mood when he got the report. So he ordered me to find one pure soul to replace the one I'd lost. We had words. I insulted him. Then, boom! Here I am. A mortal." Wincing, he added, "I don't know how you do it, Gemma. How are you able to be mortal when it's so confusing and painful?"

She took another sip of her coffee, her eyes never leaving him. "Okay. Let's say you find that one pure soul. Then what?"

He shrugged. "I guess I get my old job back."

"How long will that take?"

"I don't know. I really, honestly, can't tell you."

She turned her face to glance out the window again. In the diffused sunlight, her skin took on a creamy, almost porcelain-like texture. Smooth and unblemished, except for the light dappling of freckles. Danelius swallowed hard. Such beauty was rare to come by.

"Okay. Let's get this straight between us." She turned

back to him. He could sense she still didn't quite believe him, but at least she was willing to give him some leeway.

"I still think your story is shit, but I can't help but believe you. Either you are the most consummate actor who's never won an Oscar, or there's a grain of truth to this cockamamie tale. The weather is too terrible to send you away, so here's what I propose. You can stay here until the weather breaks and the roads reopen. But as soon as that happens, you're out of here. I don't care if you have to walk out wearing those sweatpants and t-shirt. You got me?"

Danelius nodded. There was nothing he could say.

She flashed him a smile. "Good. Now that we got that over with, and I can't go in to work, I guess we're stuck with each other's company. Let's see if there's a good movie on the television. We might as well take advantage of the electricity while we have it."

She got up from the table and began taking items to the sink. He was still confused about what he had agreed to, but at least he understood that she was letting him remain with her, at least for a little longer. But who was electricity, and how was he supposed to take advantage of it?

CHAPTER FIVE

They were both still hungry, so she made more cinnamon rolls out of a can, and they ate them with more cups of coffee as they watched some movie on a sheet of glass. The movie was almost over when all the lights went dark, including the movie, and Gemma groaned.

"Well, that was inevitable."

"What was?"

She got up from the couch. Outside, snow clouds blanketed the sky as they readied to drop their load. The light coming through the windows was dank and gray, but it was enough to see by, just not clearly. She fumbled around, opening and closing drawers and cabinet doors until she found what she was looking for. Gemma lit a candle. "It's not much, but it'll help some. Let's go into the kitchen."

Without waiting for his answer, she turned and left the living room. Danelius grabbed the plate of remaining rolls and followed her. She was delving into a drawer. Soon, she withdrew a small box and tossed it on the table as he sat down.

"Ever play poker?"

"Poke her?" He stared at the box. How did fornicating have anything to do with the object on the table?

Gemma took the chair next to him. She had found two more candles, which she lit and sat upright on a small plate, next to the other candle. Grabbing the box, she emptied it, and a multitude of slender sheets of hard parchment slid into her hand.

"Not 'poke her'. Poker. Never mind. I'll teach you how to play fish. Ever play cards before?"

"Cards?"

"Yeah."

"What are cards?"

"Never mind. We'll start from the beginning."

She scooted her chair closer to him, until he could

sense her heat. Unconsciously, he reached over and rubbed a sleeve from her pajamas between two fingers.

"You're warm."

"Yeah." She giggled softly. "It's not every day I can spend the day in my jammies, but this is going to be one of them, to be sure. All right. These are cards." She held up the small sheets of hard parchment and proceeded to tell him about the game they were going to play with the sheets, but at that point Danelius only paid partial attention to her instructions.

He could feel her heat, but he could also sense more. There was a warm, womanly fragrance surrounding her like a cloud. He enjoyed the way her skin shimmered in the candlelight. Her dark hair changed from red to gold, depending on the way the flames danced. A familiar tightening in his groin let him know there was something about this woman that made her unlike any of the others he had encountered. Something that affected him in ways he couldn't fathom.

He had lost his ability to make himself inflate his erection. All of his supernatural powers had been nullified the moment he landed her in mortal form. So how was she able to make him feel so omnipotent again?

"Dan? Yoo-hoo."

He dragged his attention away from studying her, and looked into her eyes.

"You haven't heard a word I said, have you?"

"I do not understand what is happening, Gemma."

"What do you mean?"

"I'm not immortal anymore. I can't seduce anyone. I can't even get my cock to cooperate when I want it to. I thought...I thought I had lost all interest in sex."

"You *thought* you had?"

"Look!" He reared back and pulled down his pants where she could see his growing erection. "I'm not doing it, but I am! I mean, it's doing it by itself!"

"They usually do, Dan." Her comment was laced with amusement, giving him the impression she was laughing at him.

"No, you still don't understand. All throughout my existence, I have had to fuck women in order to cement their souls to the devil. It was my job, condemning them. I went to them in their dreams and I became the person they wanted me to be, and I fucked them. There was no thought to what I did. Each day I did what I was told, and when I did a good job, I was allowed to do it again the next day."

By this time he had her full attention. She laid the pieces of plastic parchment on the table and listened.

"There were no feelings involved. I cared nothing for the women I was told to fuck. I cared nothing for their lives. I cared nothing about fucking!"

"You cared nothing about fucking, but you did it day in and day out without rest for years?"

"Eons. Millennia. I don't remember."

"So, what are you trying to tell me, Dan?"

He shook his head. "I don't know. I know the Old Man kicked me out of Hell because I failed my last mission. I know he ordered me to bring him back a pure soul if I wanted to get my job back. And then he dumped me here, where I found you."

He looked up, into her eyes now dark in the candlelight. "I think I care about you, Gemma. And that's why my body is responding like this when I'm with you."

Her smile was almost luminescent. "I think I care about you, too, Dan. You're an odd person to figure out. Okay. Scratch that. You're just plain odd. And quirky. And different. But there's something about you that I like. I don't know why. You're nothing like the type of guys I'm normally attracted to. But you..."

Her smile broadened. Suddenly, she leaned toward him, cocked her head to one side, and pressed her lips to his. Danelius nearly fell out of his chair in shock.

"What was that for?" He touched his mouth with the tips of his fingers. The sensation remained. He could still feel her lips. Their warmth and wetness. "What did you do?"

"It's a kiss. Don't you know what a kiss is?"

"Yes, I know what a kiss is, but it's not like that. I mean, it's never been like that."

"Never been like what?" She was almost laughing at him again. Almost.

Pulling out the waistband of his sweatpants again, he stared at the transformation. "I must have grown another inch!"

"Dan, are you saying you've never been turned on by a kiss?" She propped her head in her hand, and her elbow on the table.

"I know the perfunctories. I know the drill and the routine. But the feelings..." He touched his mouth again, remembering. "As an incubus, I was impervious to disease. Heat and cold meant nothing to me. If by some circumstance an arrow or sword or bullet went through me, I remained uninjured. Nothing touched me. Nothing *could* touch me."

"All that's changed now, hasn't it?" she murmured. "You can feel cold. You can suffer from its effects. But, at the same time, you can feel what soft is. What hunger and thirst is."

"Yes."

"And you can understand happiness."

He glanced up from where he had been watching the barely moving candle flame. She was waiting for him to reply.

"Happiness?"

"Yeah. It comes from when the body and mind are content. When there are no worries, nothing to detract from enjoying what you're seeing or hearing. Or doing."

"Like now."

Gemma smiled. The candle flame showed off her white teeth. "Are you happy at this moment, Dan?"

"Yes." Yes, he was. Very happy, in fact. The self-confession surprised him. "I'm happy...because of you."

"Me?" She laughed softly and shook her head. Her hair glimmered where it fell around her shoulders. Impulsively, he reached out and brushed some of it over her back.

"Yes. You. If it weren't for you, I would be gone by now."

"Bull hockey. Satan wouldn't let you die if you still

owed him."

"Not die. Gone. Non-existing. Incubi aren't born. We're created. We exist only as long as we're needed, then we're dismissed. Most of the time, if we fail our duty, we're gone. It's a very rare instance when someone like me is given a second chance to redeem himself."

"You must be exceptional at what you do."

He started to nod, then stopped. "I am. I mean, I was. But I think there has to be another reason why I was allowed this amount of leniency."

"Which is?"

"I don't know."

She looked at him, silently evaluating what he told her. "So, what you're telling me is that this is your final chance to prove yourself, or face a true death, right?"

A true death. Although the words meant nothing to him, the thought they conveyed still managed to send a shiver throughout his body.

"Are you cold?"

"No. No. Just..."

"Never mind. I understand." She placed a warm hand over his, sending another stream of desire pouring through him. He squeezed back and somehow managed a smile.

"Is there a time limit when you have to present this pure soul to Hades?" she asked.

"I'm not sure. Time normally isn't regarded in Hell."

"And what would the devil consider to be a pure soul? Like a virgin?"

"I guess. I don't know. Someone without any indiscretions coloring their past. Someone who has not done evil or wrong to others."

"You mean someone who hasn't broken any of God's commandments?"

Dan grimaced. "The G word isn't spoken where I come from. It's taboo."

She smiled. "Sorry."

"That's all right. It's not like I haven't heard it before."

Another thought came to him. An uglier thought, and one that almost froze him to the core. "Gemma, are you a pure soul? Are you the pure soul I was meant to take?"

His trepidation began to turn into a rancid boil in his stomach at the idea, when Gemma leaned back in her chair. Her laughter was louder and more boisterous. "Me? Pure? Oh, give me a break!"

The acidic flume began to settle. "You're certain you're not pure? I have to know, Gemma!"

"Hell, I haven't been a virgin since I was eighteen. And as for not breaking any of G— Sorry. Breaking any commandments, you can throw that right out the window, too. I've lied. I've coveted. I've even stolen. Hell, I've probably broken half of them."

Relief washed through him. She wasn't pure. Which meant the awful, terrifying thought that she may be the person Satan wanted him to procure was nonsense.

But it also meant that the pure soul was still out there, out in the mortal world, and he had to find that person. Soon. The Old Man wasn't exactly the patient sort. A gentle shove to his shoulder drew him out of his thoughts.

"Then, let me get this straight. You screw women for a living, but it means nothing to you. You get no pleasure from it. You aren't happy in your job, but you're okay with that. How am I doing so far?"

"I would say that's a pretty good summary of what I do."

"You've never made love and gotten enjoyment out of it?"

He gave her an inquisitive look. "You mean people enjoy fucking?"

Gemma suddenly got to her feet, still holding onto his hand, and started to drag him out of his own chair. "Come on."

"Why? Where?"

She pulled him out of the kitchen and into the living room. When they reached the entrance to the hallway, he stopped her. "Where are you taking me?"

"To my bedroom."

"Gemma."

"Shut up. I've done nothing but think about this all

night. *You're* definitely interested, so why not? Let's go and get this out of our system before we drive each other nuts."

He stumbled and almost fell onto the floor in her haste to drag him into the bedroom. "Wait. Wait, Gemma. Is this wise?"

"Wise?" She gave him an incredulous look. "This coming from an ex-demon?"

"I...I..."

Her eyes widened. "What are you trying to tell me, Dan?"

"I don't know how to..."

"You don't know how to what? How to make love?"

The phrase hung between them like an invisible door, with her on one side and he on the other.

Make love.

"No. I don't know how to make love. I know how to fuck, but..."

"Want to learn how?" she gently asked, giving his hand a squeeze. It was as if she'd wrapped her fingers around his cock and was starting to manipulate it. Had he been his demon self, he would have pounced upon her right there in the hallway and screwed her senseless. But the idea of making love to her...

"Is making love that much different?"

"Mmm, let's just say you get a lot more out of it. Trust me, Dan. As a mortal, you're going to enjoy it."

Danelius took a deep breath. "Well, hell, what do I have to lose?"

Before Gemma could respond, he rushed past her and practically dragged her into the bedroom.

CHAPTER SIX

This was crazy. No, it was sheer lunacy. She wasn't that kind of girl. What's more, if someone had told her a week ago that she'd find some idiot wandering around in his birthday suit on a freezing cold night, take him home, and screw him, she would have laughed herself silly.

Now look at her.

But she couldn't deny the fact that the man made her horny. God, he was built like an Adonis, attractive as any movie star, and, above all, *hung*. Add in his sweet sincerity, and that cock-and-bull story about being kicked out of hell, plus being iced in by the weather, and she was looking at one long day thinking about nothing but taking the guy for a test drive.

All right. Give the man credit for making his tale so absurd, it sounded like the synopsis for a movie. Yet, for all its absurdity, she knew the man was harmless. She would swear her life on it.

Maybe he was a nut job who got loose from the funny farm, and a good-looking one at that! Maybe he was suffering from amnesia. No telling how long he'd been wandering in the dark before she nearly ran him over.

But the man was putting out some serious sexual vibes, whether he knew it or not. It was all she could do to keep her legs crossed and her hands off of him, until she realized it was a losing battle.

Plus, Dan was certainly interested in her. Which made her decision that much easier.

He half-dragged her into the bedroom. Pulling him around until he stood in front of her, she released his hand and shoved him backwards onto the bed. He bounced slightly, his legs bending over the end of the mattress, but he never took his eyes off of her. While he watched and waited, she pulled her pajama top over her head, baring her breasts. Immediately, his gaze dropped to them, and to her delight, widened.

'You said you've never had fun fucking a woman. And ı't know what making love is about. Are you willing to ɪɪnɑ oʋʈ?"

He nodded silently.

"Well, then, strip!"

To his credit, he was out of his two items of clothing in the same amount of time it took for her to divest herself of her bottoms. His cock, unfettered, stood straight up like a soldier at attention. A soldier with a leaky hat.

One look at the thick pole with veins pulsing on the sides, and Gemma dropped to her knees at the end of the bed. She took the muscle into both hands and squeezed. Danelius jumped slightly.

"What's the matter?"

"What are you doing?" he whispered.

"I'm going down on you," she whispered back, adding an impish grin. "Haven't you had someone do a blow job on you?"

As she half-expected, he looked puzzled. "Blow job?"

"How about a sixty-nine?"

"I'm not following you."

"Forget it. That's lesson two. Or maybe three."

Before he could ask what lesson one was, she first nuzzled his crotch, letting her breath tickle the sensitive skin. Was that lavender she smelled? Satisfied, she bent over the flushed head and carefully inserted it into her mouth.

Danelius nearly shot off the bed. "Gemma!"

Rather than reply, she gave his cock a squeeze as she moved one hand to his generously-sized balls. Like the rest of his body, his pubic area had no hair. In fact, she could feel no hint of stubble, and wondered if he got himself waxed. Did men get their testicles waxed? Did they go into a salon and say, "I'd like a wax job on my nuts."? A little voice in her head played out the scenario with the proprietor replying, "Yes, sir. And today we have a two-for-one special." At the accompanying visual, she almost choked on him with laughter.

Regardless, she could feel his dick pulsing with a

CAROLYN GREGG

strong beat in her hands. The head was incredibly soft and firm inside her mouth, and she licked it vigorously. Danelius groaned. She took it for a good sign, and shifted tactics. Gently scraping the sides of his erection with her teeth, she felt his cock grow even hotter in her hand. That was her signal to begin pumping him, squeezing with her fingers as her hand went down, then tugging on the skin when she pulled back up. Squeeze, then pull. Pressing, then tugging. She found the smooth patch of skin underneath his balls, directly between his legs, and felt for the sperm duct. Finding it, she pressed down, knowing it was an erogenous zone for him, and Danelius squirmed from the sensation.

As she manipulated him, her mouth pumped him up and down. Another droplet oozed from the rounded head, and she slowly licked it off, adding a hard suck at the end. Danelius reached down to grab her hair.

"I'm...I'm..." His face was twisted, his eyes almost rolled back in his head.

"You like?"

She twirled her tongue around the rim of the head, using the tip to tease underneath the helmet's fold. The cock quivered in her hand, and she knew he was about to explode. She grabbed the nearest thing at hand, the t-shirt he'd thrown off, and covered his dick with it. His erection pulsed hard several times as he ejaculated, each time accompanied by a grunt and a shudder. When he was done, Gemma removed the shirt and wiped him off before tossing the piece of clothing onto the floor.

"Don't tell me that was your first orgasm."

"It was..." He swallowed noisily. "Unbelievable."

"Good! I'm glad you liked. Now it's your turn to do me."

He barely managed to raise his head and turn to look at her. She could tell he was still swimming in the sea of sweet release, as she liked to think of it.

"Do you?" He glanced down at his now-partially deflated cock. The head was drooping slightly to one side, giving it a candy cane appearance. He looked back at her. "How?"

"I don't mean screwing me, Dan. I meant eating me."

His confusion vanished with an "Oh!" and he immediately scooted to the end of the bed. Rolling onto his stomach, he grabbed her thighs and pulled her toward his mouth. Gemma covered herself with one hand.

"Nope. Not yet. I want a little foreplay first."

"Foreplay?"

"Do you know what foreplay is, Dan? Like kissing, or teasing my nipples?"

"I normally just go for it. Straight and simple."

"Then you're missing out. Okay, I'll give you directions. You just follow them. Got it?"

"Just tell me where."

"To begin with, let's scoot up. You'll *end* at my pussy."

He stared at her swollen pubic lips, and from the look on his face she could tell this was going to be a whole new adventure for him.

"Dan?"

He looked back up at her.

"We're just getting started. I hope you have the stamina to finish this, because I haven't had a really good rogering in ages."

"Will it feel anything like what I just went through?" he asked with a grin.

"Oh, yeah. You can bet on it," she promised. "Now, come up here and start by sucking on my tits."

CHAPTER SEVEN

There was something hellaciously erotic about teaching someone like Dan how to make love. It was also oddly funny that she would have to show an incubus how to please a woman. It wasn't that he was ignorant of the finer details. It was the fact that he had never experienced the simple, sexy joy of fooling around before going for the hardcore action.

After a few seconds of him tugging on her nipple like it was a rubber band, Gemma realized she needed to be a lot more patient. Unfortunately, patience was the smallest portion on her plate at the moment.

Her body was silently screaming for completion. She was so wet, she could feel herself oozing between her thighs. To make matters worse, his cock was planted between her legs, with the firm head nudging her pubes. She wriggled her hips, and he responded with a little shove. It was taking all of her willpower not to just go ahead and spread her thighs, and let him plunge on in.

A spark of pain lanced through her breast. Grabbing his face, she carefully detached his mouth.

"Ouch. Whoa. It's a nipple, Dan. Not a rubber toy."

"Sorry."

Knowing it would be useless to suggest he suck on it like a baby, she tried a different tactic. "Lick it. Slowly. Pretend it's something delicious to eat, and you want to savor it as long as possible."

She watched him drag his tongue from the bottom of her breast, over the swell, and across the nipple. It was a unique experience for her, watching a man give her pleasure. In the past she'd always kept her eyes closed, believing that her other senses would heighten the pleasure.

Her assumption had been wrong.

Danelius kept eye contact with her as he twirled the tip of his tongue around the areola, the same way she had done to the crown of his penis. Giving the hard little tip several flicks, he closed his lips over the end and sucked on it like a straw.

Raw hunger surged through her. She arched her back and gasped, unable to stop him because he was holding her wrists down on the mattress. She felt cold air on her wet breast, and then his mouth began to do the same thing to her other one. Midway around her tightening bud, he surrounded it with his lips and began to hum. Curious, she started to wonder what he was up to, but that thought was drowned in the vibrations working through her, tingling and tickling all the way to her core. At some point she must have made a sound, because Danelius paused.

"Am I doing it right?"

She was barely able to gasp an answer. "Oh, yeah. Oh, yes."

He released her wrists and started to move down her body, mouthing and kissing her skin an inch at a time. Skimming over her belly and ribs, and taking care not to miss anything. Sometimes he would lick, making her flesh go all goose-pimply. His warm breath made her shiver. His lips and tongue left wet trails that turned cold. Gemma lifted her hips, and Danelius chuckled.

"This is fun."

She couldn't answer him. He was prodding her belly button with his tongue. His manipulations felt like matches striking phosphorous. Hot sparks ignited nerve endings, seared paths across muscles, until they pooled to sizzle inside her pussy.

"More."

The word came from somewhere. It couldn't have come from her. But Danelius obliged with long, slow licks, starting from her hipbones and ending at the trimmed patch above her pubes. Playfully, he tugged on the short curls with his lips, then nuzzled her. Before she had the chance to open her legs wider, he separated the labia with his fingers.

"Want me to lick this, too?"

"Dan!"

His chuckle puffed heat across her sensitive skin. She

writhed beneath him, her legs trapped by his weight. At least her hands were free—or so she thought until she reached down to bury her fingers in his hair. He grabbed her wrists again and held them down.

"Don't stop me," he nearly growled, and burrowed his face between her thighs.

She couldn't take the intense sensations blooming inside her. His attempts were clumsy, awkward, but they worked to his advantage. His tongue slid over her pulsing skin and sucked at the cream that continued to coat the inner lips. Hot, rough, and large, it was a living vibrator lighting fires under her body, and melting her into a puddle of flesh. His grip on her wrists, and his weight on her legs, prevented her from throwing his off. They also kept her from moving around, making the delightful torture more intense. She was gasping for air now. Her sweat-coated body was one massive erogenous zone, riding on the cusp.

"Dan!"

His head jerked up. "What? Am I hurting you?"

"Fuck me. Oh, please. Now. I'm so close."

He was instantly on his knees, and spreading hers. Despite her lust-fogged mind, she somehow managed to pat him, then point toward the bedside table.

"Condoms. There."

Her request caught him by surprise. She heard the drawer open and close, but after a long moment of no further movement on the bed, Gemma opened her eyes. Danelius was holding up the long connected strand of individual condoms like a flat, uncoiled rope.

"Oh, for heaven's sake."

She snatched the packets from his hand and tore one off, throwing the rest onto the floor beside the bed. She worked swiftly, fearful that the initial glow he'd worked up in her would diminish.

Once she tore open the packet and extracted the condom, she grabbed his arrow-straight erection and tugged on it. "Come here."

He shuffled forward on his knees and watched in amazement as she rolled the glove down his length. When she was done, she patted the top of his thigh.

"All right. Now show me what you've got, big boy."

This time there was no awkwardness, no clumsiness, no hesitancy. Danelius gradually worked his thick cock into her, giving her body time to adjust to the size of the head tunneling into her. When she felt his scrotum nestle against her lower lips, she shivered with anticipation.

"Now, let me show you what I've learned after thousands of years of practice," he murmured as he bent over her.

There was nothing she could say, much less think, as he moved in and out of her, starting slowly, then picking up speed and intensity with every stroke. Some kind of connection must have formed between them, because the moment an idea crossed her mind, Danelius made it real. When she instinctively started to

lift her knees, he reached out and did it for her. He spread her wider without her having to do it on her own. Only once did he pause, and that was to shove a pillow underneath her buttocks.

Thick and slick, Danelius screwed her like a professional. Soon, they were both panting from their efforts. Sweat dotted their skin. Gemma cried out for more, to be ridden harder, and Danelius doubled his efforts.

Her orgasm came with a sudden fierceness that shocked her. Crying out, she reached up and managed to grasp his shoulders with both hands. Unmindful of the fact that she was digging her nails into his skin. He was ramming himself into her, pounding hard and forcefully. Rutting. Fucking. Almost animalistic. She couldn't breathe. White hot, the ecstasy plowed through her, until she nearly blacked out.

And then Danelius erupted for the second time.

CHAPTER EIGHT

His belly hurt. It tended to spasm on him, pushing inward as if an invisible fist was punching his abdomen. Painful enough to keep him from getting any further restful sleep.

Slowly, Danelius sat up and swung his legs over the side of the bed. Gemma was lying with her back to him, and for a moment he thought she was asleep until he heard her mutter.

"Wha's wrong?"

"My stomach hurts."

"Then you either need to go to the bathroom, or you need to eat something." She adjusted herself slightly and pulled the sheet up over her bare shoulder, but even in mortal form, he could sense her drifting back to unconsciousness.

Bathroom or kitchen. Easy enough.

He maneuvered his way through the dark into the bathroom. Unable to tell if he would hit or miss the toilet, he decided to play it safe and go in the sink. He definitely felt better after this little mission, but the hollow pit in the center of his body continued to contract. Since that one act didn't suffice, next stop, the kitchen.

He only stubbed his toe once, on the floor lamp as he entered the room containing the couch and television. As he rounded the short partition that separated that room from the kitchen, something Gemma called a bar, he reached for where he remembered the table should be. On the table were candles and matches, and he quickly lit one. Holding the votive before him, he turned to check what was inside the cold box when the small light illuminated the figure of a man seated not three feet away, by the table. At the same time he nearly jumped when he saw the intruder, the stranger spoke.

"How's mortality treating you, Danelius?"

Danelius felt his skin pucker in the cold breeze that

d to be flowing within the room, yet the candle was
ɔcted. "Hello, Torreon. To what do I owe the visit?" He
ed the man was naked, which was usual for a demon.
Despite his casual, sit-back relaxed appearance, Danelius
knew that his friend was on a mission. "Have you come by to
check up on me?"

"Partly. Actually, I'm here to finish a job."

Danelius paused with his hand on the refrigerator
handle. Something in the demon's tone sent a jagged spike of
fear up his spine. He glanced over to where Satan's minion
was still seated at the table, a knowing smile pasted on his
face. As the truth slowly uncurled its serpentine coils from
inside his gut, Danelius turned to face the creature.

"What job?"

Torreon's smile grew wider, to become a horrific
parody of joy. "The Old Man is happy with your latest
conquest. He sent me to congratulate you, and to bring both
of you back to face him."

Danelius frowned darkly. "Both of us?"

"Yes. You and the woman."

Although he'd suspected to hear something similar
coming from his friend, the announcement still sent another
shiver of fear through him.

"Why? She wasn't a pure soul. She even told me
which commandments she'd broken."

Torreon tsked as he rose to his feet and slowly shook
his head. "Danelius, Danelius, Danelius. You haven't been
keeping up with the manual, have you?"

"That frigging manual gets updated more often than I
fuck," Danelius snapped back. "Be specific!"

"A pure soul has nothing to do with how many
commandments the person has broken. It has to do with
what's in their heart. It has to do with whether or not the
person had malice or other devious purposes in mind when
the acts were committed." He threw a thumb over his
shoulder to indicate the woman sleeping in the bedroom.
"Miss Gemma MacKenzie is a pure soul. Or was, until you
fucked her."

Danelius tried to contain the anger and fear rising

inside him. "How was what we did, how did that contaminate her?"

Torreon laughed as he waved a hand in Danelius' direction. "You're a demon! She screwed a demon! That's what condemned her!"

"I'm a mortal!"

"Yes, and the Devil still owns your soul. You still belong to him."

Before Danelius could retort, Torreon began to walk around the room. "You know the rule. Condemning a pure soul to the depths of Hell is like hitting the jackpot! It's so rare, Beelzebub himself is hard pressed to accomplish such a feat. That's why he gave you this mission. He truly believed you would fail. I mean, after all, you're just a lowly little incubus. Imagine Satan's surprise, imagine *all* of us gawking in surprise, when you took that little bitch down!"

"She's not a bitch." Danelius had no idea his teeth were clenched when he spoke, but he didn't care. "And you're not taking her back with you."

Torreon stopped chuckling, but the smile remained. "Now you're talking nonsense."

"Try me."

"How do you think you're going to stop me? You're mortal. I'm not. In fact..."

The demon disappeared from view. A split-second later, Danelius heard a scream coming from the bedroom. He ran out of the kitchen, hitting his shin on the low table in front of the couch. The momentary pain cleared his head of the last remnants of clinging sleep, and he halfway slid into the bedroom to see Torreon holding a terrified Gemma in his arms. The moment he entered the room, her wide eyes cemented themselves on him. Even with Torreon's hand covering her mouth, he could hear her pleas ringing inside his skull.

"Ready?" the demon asked.

Danelius opened his mouth to beg for Gemma's sake, when the room suddenly brightened, becoming a glowing reddish-orange fireball. A wave of heat literally slammed him to the ground, and for a long moment he lay there, stunned but not disoriented. He knew where he was. He knew where Torreon had taken them.

The stench of death filled his lungs, nearly making him gag. It was a smell he had breathed for countless years, but it had never affected him like this. Not like it did now. It, along with the rancid, sulfuric smoke, made his eyes burn until tears rolled down his face. As he struggled to get to his feet, a familiar voice behind him boomed out. "Welcome back, Danelius. Congratulations on a job well done!"

His first concern was Gemma. He quickly located her, still in Torreon's grasp where they stood off to one side. It was a good sign. At least the demon hadn't already absconded with her to the depths.

Turning back around, he stared up into the face of darkness. "Let her go."

One thick, black eyebrow, like a thundercloud, rose slightly. "What?"

With that one word, Danelius felt his legs turn rubbery. No one *told* the Devil what to do. And woe be to the person who *ordered* Him. But this time Danelius knew he had no other choice. Not when it came to Gemma. This woman had changed him. Because of her, and because of his mortality, his existence had taken on a whole new meaning. His life had and would always belong to Satan. But her life... She didn't belong here, and he was determined to do whatever he needed to prevent her from spending eternity in this domain.

He glanced over at her, but his words were directed at the towering Master of Hell. "I said, let her go. I'll find you another pure soul."

Incredibly, Beelzebub chuckled. "I like this game you have created to counteract your punishment. But I am weary of it. You have completed your task."

He held out his enormous hand, palm facing Danelius. A fireball erupted from the fingertips, enveloping him with scorching flames. Strength ballooned inside him, and Danelius knew he was once more immortal. He could now fight for Gemma, although he knew there was no way he could win. As the Devil nodded at Torreon to take her below,

Danelius moved in between the Old Man and the demon he once called his friend. With his hands gripped into tight fists, Danelius lifted his chin to face Satan head-on.

"Explain something to me first." It was a flat demand. And by its tone, it brooked no argument. Behind his back, he heard Torreon's gasp of surprise.

Satan stared at him in disbelief for a handful of seconds.

Danelius knew he could never defeat the Old Man. His powers were miniscule compared to the Master's. But Danelius also knew the Devil liked surprises, especially those which entertained him, however briefly.

"Explain what?"

"Explain why, if she was a pure soul, she's now condemned."

"Because she had carnal knowledge of you!" a voice hissed behind his back.

The Old Man nodded slightly. "Exactly. She knew you were a demon, yet she deliberately gave herself to you *without remorse.* "

"I gave myself to him because I love him!"

Everyone looked to see Gemma, still struggling in Torreon's hold, but with her mouth no longer covered. A single nod from Satan, and the demon released his grip. Gemma stood there, defiance on her sweat-stained face. Like the rest of them, she was completely nude. But unlike them, her body glistened with perspiration. Even with her hair mussed and flying around her face and shoulders, she was more beautiful than anything Danelius had ever seen.

"You're right," she continued. "I have no remorse for what I did. For what we did. And you know why? Because I love him. Because I've developed sincere feelings for him. I don't care if he's a demon. I don't care what he's done in the past. We made love. We didn't screw. We didn't fuck. We. Made. Love. If that condemns me to eternity in Hell, so be it."

To show her commitment, she walked up to join Danelius, taking his hand in hers. She flashed him a weak but sincere smile before Danelius turned back to Satan.

"Let me go with her."

At first, Satan stared uncomprehending at him. The leepened on the Old Man's face as he gave a deep rumbling growl of disapproval. "I believe this joke has gone far enough, but it has been amusing. Inasmuch, I will allow you to escort her into the depths, but you cannot remain. I need you to resume your position. There is work to do."

Gemma turned and buried her face in Danelius' shoulder. He could feel her tears burning where they hit his skin. Her voice was soft.

"Oh, God, I'm sorry."

The Devil reacted as if he had been hit with a bucket of ice water.

"What? What is she doing?"

"Forgive me, Dan. Forgive me for not believing you. I'm sorry for this trouble I'm putting you though. God forgive me, but I do love you."

"No, no, no." Satan wagged his finger at them. Dark, vicious clouds formed overhead, blackening a nonexistent ceiling. "Stop what you're doing. *Stop what you're doing!* "

Danelius touched her face with his fingertips and tried to shush her. "It's all right, Gemma. I forgive you. I'm just sorry you had to be the one to be punished."

She hiccupped slightly and raised her eyes to his. "If loving you is a sin, I can accept that. But it won't stop me from loving you."

He reached for her, wrapping his arms around her one final time. Holding her tightly against him.

Love. This was what love felt like. This need to protect her, to give himself in lieu of her, this was love. It wasn't just the sex. It was also the casual talk in the kitchen. The watching of a movie in companionable silence. It was the laughter, the bickering, and the misunderstanding. As alien as the emotion felt within his chest, it didn't hurt. In fact, it glowed.

"And I love you, Gemma."

"God help us both," she murmured as their lips met.

"*Stop this! Stop it now!* " The voice was a thunderclap, nearly breaking their eardrums. Danelius and

Gemma clutched their ears against the pain.

"I will not have her invoking his name in here! Take her below now!"

Lifting her tear-stained face, Gemma looked directly at the monstrous horror before her. "I hope one day God forgives you, too," she solemnly stated.

Satan screamed.

And Hell disappeared.

CHAPTER NINE

An enormous weight pressed down on his back. Breathing was a struggle, and he fought to draw air into his lungs.

He lay flat on his stomach with his nose smashed firmly into something soft but smothering. As he struggled, a foot placed itself on his butt cheeks and shoved down hard, grinding his pelvis and privates into the floor. What little air he'd managed to inhale came out in a grunt.

"Well, I hope you're happy."

Danelius peeled his eyes open and blinked. The world no longer pulsed blood-red. The distant screams were gone, replaced by intense silence. And the heat...

He shuddered from the cold. They weren't in Hell anymore, but he bet he could figure out where they'd been sent in three guesses or less.

The pressure on his buttocks let up. Rolling over, he stared up at the demon glowering down at him. "Happy about what?"

"Permanent exile. You've been kicked out for good, old friend."

There was a cough and the sound of movement coming from behind him. Danelius rose up on his elbows, enough to turn his head and look back. To his relief, he saw Gemma roll onto her side.

She paused when she spotted him. In the next instant, she lifted her eyes up to the demon towering over them. "Kicked out?" Her voice was raspy, probably an aftereffect from breathing in the smoke and sulfur from below.

Torreon's face twisted in disgust, but his attention remained on his former coworker. "How dare you use the G word, Danelius! You broke Satan's cardinal rule. I can't believe you'd stoop so low."

"He didn't say it," Gemma corrected. "I did."

The demon kept his back to her. "You know you'll never get another second chance from the Old Man. You're doomed. For eternity. But before that happens, you'll have to live out the rest of your short, miserable existence in mortal form." He shook his head. "I can't believe you fell to these depths."

Danelius coughed. The feeling wasn't pleasant. "I think it was inevitable."

"How?"

"I think Satan intended to kick me out sooner or later."

Torreon barked with laughter. "How do you figure?"

"He put me here in mortal form to test me."

"To test you? You said he put you here to find a pure soul so you could redeem yourself."

"He did, but it was a test. To see if I followed him as my true master."

"You always did. You have. For thousands of years." The demon frowned. "What changed? Where did you fail?"

Danelius glanced back at where Gemma was silently watching. "I failed when I fell in love with my target."

Torreon gave Danelius' buttocks another shove with his foot. "You failed because you acted like a mortal. You thought like a mortal. You still think like a mortal. No wonder you've been condemned to be mortal for the rest of your puny mortal life."

"And what happens after that?" Gemma spoke up.

Torreon finally gave her his attention. "What do you mean?"

"After he lives the life of a mortal, what happens then?"

"He'll die like all the other mortals. His flesh will rot with the worms until there is nothing left of him."

"But where will his soul go?" Gemma asked.

A perplexed look crossed the demon's face. "His soul?"

Gemma smiled. "You don't think the Devil will take him back to Hell, do you?"

"What concern of it is yours? Why do you care about

his soul?"

"I care about it, the same way I care about yours. Aren't you his friend?"

Torreon straightened up. "We *were* friends, until he chose differently."

"Then I forgive you, too, because you are his friend. I forgive you for abandoning him, because you've been swayed by a power greater than you. No matter what happens, no matter what you think or believe, you'll always be his friend."

"Was. I *was* his friend, but no more."

"No." She shook her head. "You still are. And you know how I know that?"

"Please tell me," he remarked sarcastically.

"Because you came here. After he and I were tossed out, you came anyway to see how he was doing."

Anger suffused his face. "I came to taunt him."

"No." Her smile softened. "You came to say goodbye because you know this is the last time you'll ever see him."

The redness spread from the demon's face to his neck, where the veins stood out and pulsed. Giving Danelius one final look, he stepped back. A moment later, he vanished from sight.

Danelius waited to see if Torreon would return, even though he knew the demon was gone for good. Either because of fear of pissing off the Old Man, or because he'd been ordered not to, Torreon would not risk a similar punishment. Danelius didn't blame him.

He got to his feet and reached down to help Gemma up. Her smile widened.

"Does this mean you get to stay?"

"You mean here? Or out of Hell?" He touched her face, smoothing back the sweat-drenched hair that clung to her cheeks and forehead.

"Both."

Drawing her arms around his neck, she stood on tiptoe and lifted her lips. Her nude body pressed firmly against him, and she playfully ground her pubes against his.

The kiss was sweet. For the first time, Danelius

realized what his banishment meant. He would get to stay with Gemma. He would get to love her for as long as they existed. Yes, it would only be for a few years. Mere decades. But there was one thing Torreon forgot. One very important thing.

Although he and Gemma would only be able to share a few mortal years, there remained eternity. And he had no doubt they would share that together, as well.

The kiss deepened. He could feel his cock hardening and pressing into her lower abdomen. Gemma giggled, reaching down with one hand to grasp him and give him a squeeze.

"How about another lesson, Dan? Think you're *up* to it?"

Before he could answer, she broke away from him and hurried down the hall toward the bedroom. Grinning, Danelius started to go after her when an old familiar tingling coursed through him. He looked down at his erection. Obediently, the pole of flesh obeyed his mental command, swerving left to right, up and down, then slipping in and out of his body cavity with ease. He chuckled as it rotated around and around like a propeller until he made it stop.

Stunned, he felt himself levitate off the carpet a few inches, and the truth of what had happened became clear. In his hurry to eject Danelius from Hell, Satan had forgotten to strip him of his demon powers again. And because the Old Man would never have anything more to do with him, the chances of the Devil discovering his error were practically nil. It was also a good bet that Torreon had washed his hands of his old friend, which meant the demon wouldn't find out and go back to report it.

A plaintive voice came from the bedroom. "Dan? You're wasting a good horny! Do I need to come in there and provide a little inspiration again?"

"I'm coming!" he said, and took off down the hallway in a sprint.

An incubus demon living as a mortal on earth. It would be a very interesting life, indeed.

ABOUT THE AUTHOR:

Carolyn Gregg, aka Linda Mooney, writes bestselling sweet, silly, sexy, sinful, sharp, sultry, smart, sassy, and seductive erotic romances. Stories that are sometimes a bit harder and edgier. Stories that sometimes push boundaries. Stories that contain language and circumstances not found in her alter ego's other books. But always with a touch of humor.

Linda Mooney, aka Carolyn Gregg, loves to write sensuously erotic romance with a fantasy, paranormal, or science fiction flair. Her technique is often described as being as visual as a motion picture or graphic novel. A wife, mother, and retired Kindergarten teacher, she lives in a small south Texas town near the Gulf coast where she delves into alternate worlds filled with daring exploits, adventure, and intense love.

She has numerous best sellers, including 10 consecutive certified #1s. In 2009, she was named Whiskey Creek Press Torrid's Author of the Year, and her book *My Strength, My Power, My Love* was named the 2009 WCPT Book of the Year. In 2011, her book *Lord of Thunder* was named the Epic Ebook "Eppie" Award Winner for Best Erotic Sci-Fi Romance.

For more information about Linda Mooney books and titles, and to sign up for her newsletter, please visit her website.
http://www.LindaMooney.com
http://shop.lindamooney.com

OTHER BOOKS BY CAROLYN GREGG

Chicken Fried Beefcake
Do Wah Diddy Me
Fits Like a Glove
The Hairy-Legged Girls Club
Hell and Damnation
La Petite Mort
The Past's Promise
The Pearl of Passion
Rhythm and Boos
Suckers
Tales of the Blakeney Sisters
      Rub My Pumpkin
      Tickle My Candy Cane
      Spank My Valentine
      Pet My Easter Bunny
      Light My Firecracker
Tit for Tat
The Virgin Sacrifice
Winter's Fyre

Made in the USA
Lexington, KY
18 January 2016